Polly Piglet

illustrated by
Francis Phillips

AWARD PUBLICATIONS LIMITED

Once upon a time there was a little piglet who lived all by herself in a big sty.

Her name was Polly Piglet, and she was round and fat and pink. She had a very funny nose that was useful for rooting about in the sty, and she had a very curly tail.

But Polly Piglet was very lonely. She peeped through the bars of her gate and saw the hens and the ducks, the lambs and the calves, and she wanted to play with them.

POLLY PIGLET

'I shall squeeze under this gate and go to play with those darling chicks,' said Polly Piglet. 'I don't like living by myself. Perhaps the hen will give me one of her chicks for my own.'

So she squeezed under the gate of her
sty. It was a very tight squeeze because
Polly was really very fat and very round.
She panted and puffed and wriggled, but
at last she managed to get through!

Polly Piglet scampered over to the
brown mother hen and her ten yellow
chicks.

'Let me play with you!' she said. 'Give
me one of your chicks for my own!'

But the yellow chicks were afraid
of Polly Piglet, and they ran away,
cheeping.

'Go away, you ugly piglet!' said the mother-hen, and she pecked poor Polly's nose.

Polly Piglet was sad. She saw the big
white mother duck nearby, and ran over
to her. The duck had eight beautiful
yellow ducklings.

'Let me play with you, please let me
play with you!' cried Polly Piglet.

But the little ducklings were afraid,
and they jumped into the pond with a
splash.

'I don't like you, ugly piglet!' quacked the big duck, and splashed Polly with water.

Splish-splash went the big drops of water, all over Polly Piglet. Some fell on her nose, some fell on her back, and some fell on her curly little tail. She didn't like it at all.

Poor Polly Piglet! She felt very sad and lonely. She walked on, and soon she saw four frisky lambs. Two had black noses, and they all had tails that wriggled and shook.

'Oh, what darlings!' cried Polly. 'How I would like one for a friend!'

She ran up to them. 'Please, little lambs, play with me,' she said. 'Do play with me. I know so many good games, and we could have fun together!'

But the lambs looked at Polly in fright. 'What is this ugly pink animal?' they bleated to one another. 'It frightens us. Let us run away!'

So they all ran away on their long legs, and their tails shook and wriggled as they went. They stood in a corner of the field and would not go near Polly Piglet.

She was very upset. Her tail lost its pretty curl and hung down straight.

'Nobody wants to be friends with me,' she said sadly. 'I am alone and by myself, and I don't like it a bit.'

Polly Piglet went on her way, looking for somebody else to talk to. Soon she saw two dear little red-and-white animals, with big brown eyes.

'They are baby cows!' said Polly to herself. 'Little calves! How sweet they look! I am sure they would love to be friends with a little pig like me.'

So she ran up to the little calves, and spoke to them in her piggy voice. 'I am very lonely,' she said. 'I have no one to play with. Please be friends with me. Won't you come and live in my sty? It is big enough for all of us!'

The little calves looked at Polly out of their soft brown eyes. One of them swung his tail round him to swish off a fly.

'What! Live with a strange-looking pig-let like you!' said the calves. 'No thank you!' And they stamped in a big brown puddle, and splashed a lot of mud all over poor Polly Piglet.

'Now you are a funny spotted pig!' they said.

So Polly had to go to the stream and wash all the mud off because she didn't like being dirty.

Polly Piglet ran on, and then she came to where some children were playing games together. There was a baby in a pram, wearing a big bonnet. She looked very sweet.

'Oh, if only she could come and live in my sty with me!' said Polly. 'I should never feel lonely then.'

So she put her front feet up on the pram and spoke to the baby.

'You are so pretty and sweet! Do come and live with me, little darling!'

But the baby was afraid of the piglet, and she cried very loudly. The other children ran up and chased the piglet away.

'How dare you make our baby cry, you ugly little pig? Go away!'

Polly was afraid of the angry children, and she trotted off quickly. The children ran after her a little way.

'Shoo, ugly little pig!' they shouted. 'Don't you dare to come near our darling baby again. If you do, we'll tell the farmer!'

'I wish I wasn't so ugly,' said poor Polly Piglet. 'If only I had feathers like the hen and the duck. If only I had soft wool like the sheep, or brown hair like the pretty calves.'

She ran on, feeling very sad. Soon she came to a clothes-line, and on it were some clean clothes belonging to the baby in the pram.

Polly looked at them. 'I have such an ugly, bare, pink body. Now, if I had pretty clothes to wear, like that baby, I should look really lovely!' Then a naughty plan came into Polly's mind. 'I will knock down this post – and the line will fall down – and the clothes will come down with it – and I will dress myself up in them!'

POLLY PIGLET

So Polly Piglet knocked down the post, and the clean clothes fell down to the ground!

What a lot there were! Coats and frocks, woollen leggings and frilly bonnets, and a really lovely red silk sash. And then little Polly Piglet had a wonderful time! First she put on a blue woollen coat. She put her front legs through the sleeves.

Then she put on some fine long woollen leggings. They fitted her back legs very well.

Then she tied a red sash round her waist, with a big bow on top of her back. She did look nice!

Last of all she put on a big bonnet, and tied the strings under her chin.

Look at her. What a pretty little piglet she is! No wonder the curl has come back to her tail.

'Perhaps everyone will like me now!' said Polly Piglet, and trotted off by herself. She really looked sweet. She was very careful not to go into any puddles because she didn't want to splash her lovely clothes. She didn't go near the hedge either, in case she caught her coat on the prickles.

'I am a very pretty little pig!' said Polly to herself.

Now, who should she meet, walking proudly along, but Mr Percy Pig! He was big and round, and Polly Piglet was afraid of him.

She tried to hide in a corner, but Mr Percy Pig saw her.

'What a lovely piglet!' he grunted. 'And how nicely dressed! Grunt-grunt-grunt – I have never seen such a ladylike pig. Where do you come from?'

'From my sty,' said Polly. 'You see, I was lonely there, and I wanted someone to play with. But nobody likes me, and they all shoo me away.'

'What a shame!' grunted kind Mr Percy Pig. 'I have always wanted a dear, pretty little wife like you. Come and live with me, and I will not let you be lonely any more.'

Oh, how happy Polly Piglet was to hear that! Now she really would have someone to love her, and to play such jolly games with her. She would never be lonely again.

She went off with Mr Percy Pig, and he told everyone how lovely she was. They met quite a lot of animals on their way to the sty.

'This is my pretty little wife,' said Mr Percy Pig to the lambs and the calves.

'This is Mrs Polly Pig, my dear little wife!' said Mr Percy Pig when they met the hen, the chicks, the duck and the ducklings.

Everyone stared at Polly, so grand in her clothes, and they nodded and bowed politely.

'How do you do? We are so pleased to meet you! Do play with us sometimes,' they all said.

'Oh, I will, I will,' Polly Piglet said happily. 'But I shan't be lonely now I have dear Mr Percy Pig to look after me.'

She trotted all through the farmyard in her new clothes, and even old Dobbin, the horse, spoke to her. 'Good morning, my lady-pig, what a pleasure to see you looking so lovely!'

POLLY PIGLET

'I am really very proud of you,' said Mr Percy Pig to Polly.

And now little Polly Piglet is so happy. She can't possibly be lonely any more because she has nine tiny pink piglets of her very own to play with.

The hen brings her little chicks to see them every day. 'Cluck-cluck!' she says. 'Your piglets are very sweet.'

'Cheep-cheep!' say the chicks. 'We want to play with them.'

The duck brings her yellow ducklings. 'Quack-quack! What beautiful piglets!' she says, and all the ducklings run into the sty to talk to the piglets.

POLLY PIGLET

The four lambs come, too, and they put their little noses through the bars of the sty-gate. 'Oh, please, Mrs Polly Pig, will you let your piglets play with us this morning?' they bleat. 'Baa-aa-baa, we do like them so!'

The two calves look over the gate and moo softly. 'What a beautiful family!' they say, gazing at them out of soft brown eyes. 'You're not lonely now, are you, Polly Piglet? You have so many piglets to play jolly games with!'

POLLY PIGLET

Even the children come and peep at the happy little family. They bring the baby and let her see the squealing piglets. She claps her hands and crows for joy.

'You don't feel unhappy now, do you, Polly?' the children say.

'Oh no. I'm the happiest pig in all the world, and I'm never lonely now!' says Polly. 'But I do wish I hadn't grown out of the lovely clothes I wore when I first met dear Mr Percy Pig!'

'Grunt-grunt! You looked very beautiful then,' says kind Mr Percy Pig, 'and you still look lovely to me, though now you only wear your skin, and have no red silk sash tied round your middle!'

ISBN 0-86163-773-9

Text copyright Darrell Waters Limited
Illustrations copyright © 1996 Award Publications Limited

Enid Blyton's signature is a trademark of Darrell Waters Limited

First published 1943 by Brockhampton Press

This edition first published 1996 by Award Publications Limited,
27 Longford Street, London NW1 3DZ

Printed in Italy